Excellent!
©Disney
Perfect work!
©Disney
You're a star!
©Disney
Well done!
©Disney
Magical effort!
©Disney
I love to read!
©Disney
Let's have fun!
©Disney
Well done!
©Disney
You deserve a reward!
©Disney
Excellent!
©Disney
Good effort!
©Disney
Reading is fun!
©Disney
Take your time
©Disney
Well done!
©Disney
A sparkling effort!
©Disney
Good work!
©Disney
Word perfect!
©Disney
Let's have fun!
©Disney
Well done!
©Disney
You deserve a reward!
©Disney
Great reading!
D0227742

STEPS TO READING

Dear Parent:

Congratulations! Your child is taking
the first steps on an exciting journey.
The destination? Independent reading!

STEPS TO READING will help your child get there. The programme offers three steps to reading success. Each step includes fun stories and colourful art, and the result is a complete literacy programme with something for every child.

Learning to Read, Step by Step!

1 **Start to Read   Nursery – Preschool**
• big type and easy words • rhyme and rhythm • picture clues
For children who know the alphabet and are eager to begin reading.

2 **Let's read together   Preschool – Year 1**
• basic vocabulary • short sentences • simple stories
For children who recognise familiar words and sound out new words with help.

3 **I can read by myself   Years 1-3**
• engaging characters • easy-to-follow plots • popular topics
For children who are ready to read on their own.

STEPS TO READING is designed to give every child a successful reading experience. The year levels are only guides. Children can progress through the steps at their own speed, developing confidence in their reading, no matter what their year.

Remember, a lifetime love of reading starts with a single step!

By Melissa Lagonegro
Illustrated by Niall Harding

This edition published by Parragon in 2011

Parragon
Queen Street House
4 Queen Street
Bath BA1 1HE, UK

ISBN 978-1-4454-2113-1

Printed in Malaysia

Ballerina Princess

Parragon

Bath • New York • Singapore • Hong Kong • Cologne • Delhi
Melbourne • Amsterdam • Johannesburg • Auckland • Shenzhen

A princess loves
to dream
about dancing.

She spins.

She twirls.

She moves
as if she is
floating on air.

Snow White meets a handsome prince.

The happy couple dances and spins.

What a lovely pair!

Belle has sweet dancing dreams.

Belle stands
on her toes.
She holds her
arms high.

She leaps

into the air.

Belle shines
like a star.
Her dress sparkles.

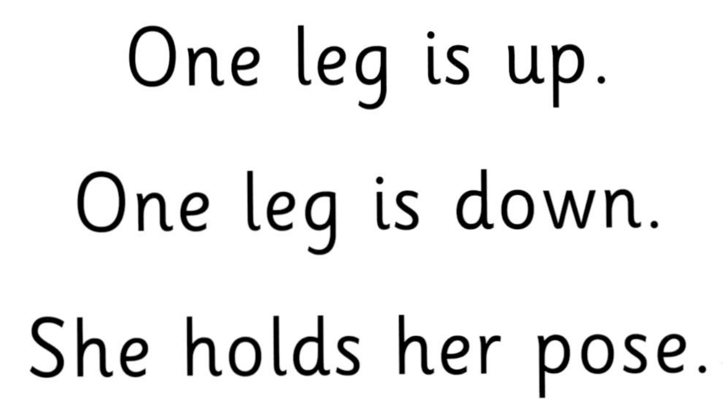

One leg is up.

One leg is down.

She holds her pose.

Aurora daydreams about her dancing costume.

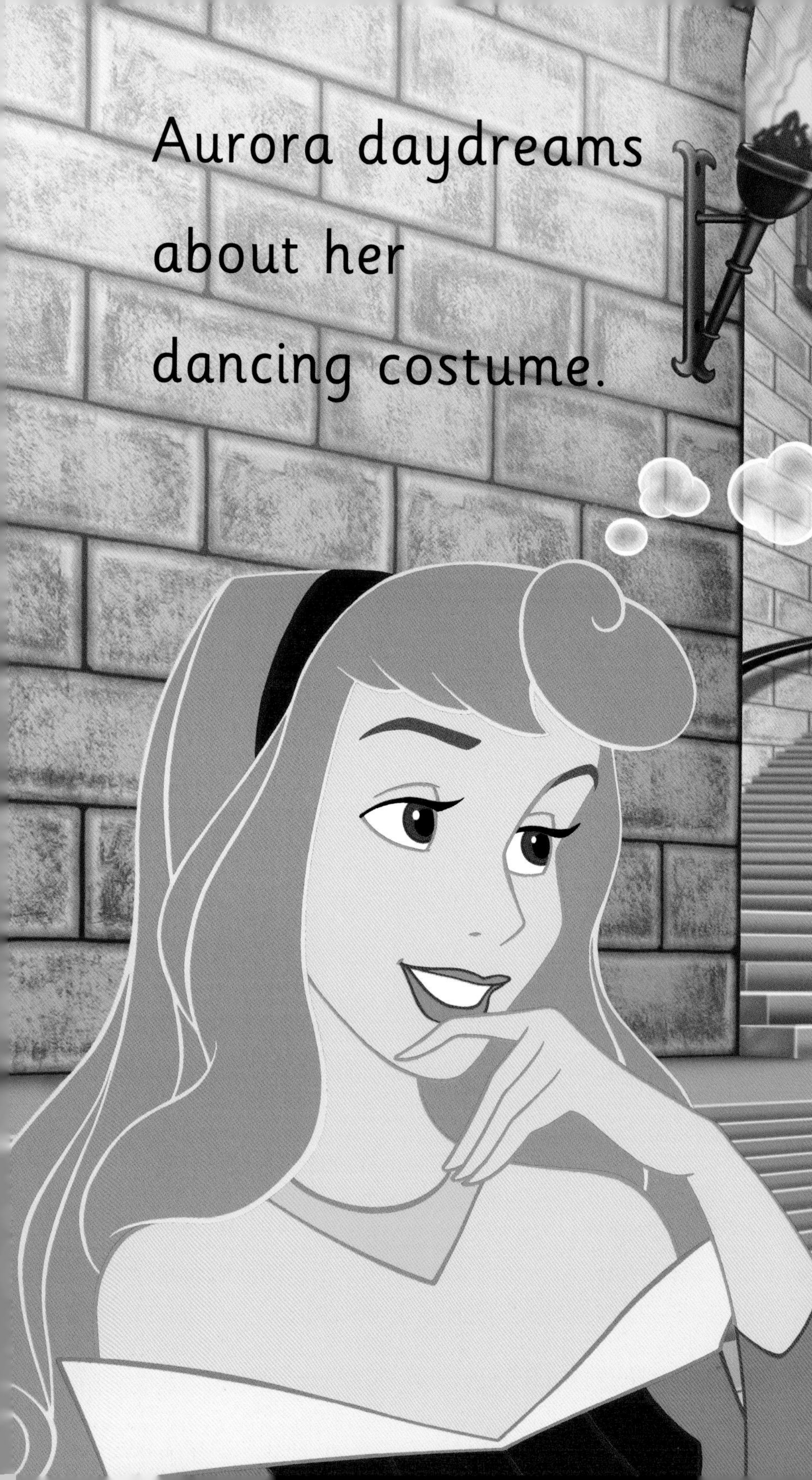

Should she wear
a tutu or a gown?

Cinderella dances
at the royal ball
in her dreams.

She twirls and whirls across the floor.

Prince Charming watches Cinderella.

The Prince takes her hand.
He asks her to dance.

They glide
across the room.
The guests
clap and cheer.

Ariel dreams
about dancing
with Prince Eric.
If only she had feet!

Spin and twirl

and jump!

Turn and leap
and prance!

A princess loves to dance!

Now turn
over for the
next story...

By Apple Jordan
Illustrated by Francesco Legramandi

Let's read together

STEPS TO READING 2

A Fairy Tale Fall

Bath • New York • Singapore • Hong Kong • Cologne • Delhi
Melbourne • Amsterdam • Johannesburg • Auckland • Shenzhen

Halloween is here!
Snow White's
friends dress up.

Happy is a prince.

Grumpy is a bear.

Sleepy is a ghost.

Boo! Roar! Howl!

A princess's haunted house is full of fun!

Belle and the Beast

pick pumpkins.

There are so many
perfect pumpkins!
They look for
the best ones.

Belle brings
her pumpkins home.
She roasts the seeds.
She bakes a pumpkin pie.

Then she carves

the biggest pumpkin.

Sleeping Beauty goes for a walk.
Her forest friends join her.

Bright leaves fall

from the trees.

Sleeping Beauty brings a picnic to share.

Pumpkin muffins and cider are tasty treats!

Jasmine wants
a new costume.
She wants one
that is perfect
for a princess!

Jasmine and Aladdin
take a ride
on the Magic Carpet.

They give treats
to all their friends!

Ariel and her friends have a costume party.

Everyone wears
a fancy mask.
No one knows
who is who!

Ariel and Flounder ride the tail of a whale.

Sebastian swims
into a seaweed forest.
Halloween is fun
under the sea!

Tiana leads
a Halloween parade.
She rides
on a spooky float.

Everyone cheers
for the royal parade.

The music is loud.
Ghosts and goblins
move to the beat!

Tonight is
the royal ball.

Cinderella makes
costumes for
all her friends.
Jaq is excited!

The Fairy Godmother makes sure the pumpkin carriage is ready.

Bibbidi-bobbidi-boo!

Fall is the perfect time for a pumpkin ride!